How I Cracked the Zodiac's Code

Melissa Brooks

Melissa Brooks

4

DEDICATION

"I dedicate my story to those who have supported me on this journey: My loving parents, whose unwavering encouragement and guidance has meant the world to me."

"I dedicate my story to those who have been impacted by the man who calls himself 'The Zodiac'. This story is for the families who have suffered unimaginable loss and heartbreak; may this book honor the memory of their loved ones."

6

Melissa Brooks

CONTENTS

1

ACKNOWLEDGMENTS

"I want to thank my daughters for listening to me talk about my

book for so many years and providing me with valuable

feedback and encouragement. I love you both more than life

itself."

"To K, my rock, thank you for your constant support, strength,

and

protection. You have been with me every step of the way, and I

love you."

"To TT, my dearest friend, thank you for your friendship, love,

and humor. I miss you every day."

```
H E R > 9 ⌐ J Λ V P K ⴹ I ● L T G ⊖ ⊖
N 9 + B φ ◨ ◰ D W Y · < ◨ K ⅂ ⊖
B Y ⵣ ⌐ M + u Z G W φ ⊕ L ■ ◆ H J
S 9 9 ⏃ Λ ⅂ ⏃ ◪ V ᑫ 9 O + + R K ⊖
▢ ⏃ M + ✦ ⊤ 2 ⅁ I ● F P + P ⊖ K /
9 ⏴ R Λ F ⅃ O — ◨ ◰ C ⅀ F > ● D φ
■ ● + K ⟳ ◘ ⵣ ⊖ u ᑕ X 6 V · ✦ L I
φ G ● J ⅂ 2 ◩ O + ▢ N Y ✦ + ◙ L ⏃
▯ < M + 8 + Z R ● F B ⊃ Y ⏃ O ● K
— ✦ ⅂ u V + Λ J + O 9 ⏃ < F B Y —
U + R / ● ⊤ 3 I D Y B 9 ⊖ T M K O
⊖ < ⊃ ⅃ R J ⅃ ◨ ● T ⊖ M · + P B F
✦ ● ⏃ S Y Z ◼ + N I ● F B ⊃ φ ⵣ ⏃ R
⅃ G F N Λ ⅂ ⊖ ● ◘ · ⊃ V ● ⊤ + +
Y B X ● ◪ ⵣ ● ⏃ C E > V u Z ⊖ — +
I ⊃ · ● ✦ B K φ O 9 Λ · ⅂ M ◰ G O
R ⊃ T + L ● ● C < + F J W B I ◆ L
+ + ⊖ W C ◆ W ⊃ P O S H T / φ ◆ 9
I F K ◰ W < ⏃ ⊤ B ◨ Y O B ■ — C ⊃
> M D H N 9 K S ✦ Z O ⏃ ⏃ I K ⵣ +
```

1 NEIGHBORS

These are the conversations and stories over the years between my friend and neighbor, Helen.

Throughout the years we passed stories back and forth on the telephone. After time we became close friends. It did not matter that we had lots of years between us. I loved Helen as if she were my blood.

It was nice to talk to my neighbor every day, she reminded me of my paternal grandmothers, but they lived on the other side of the country. Having Helen as a friend was comforting for me.

HOW I CRACKED THE ZODIAC'S CODE

Just like every grandmother, Helen loved the telephone. We talked on the phone daily. At first, we had casual conversations about our lives, the news, normal stuff people chat about. We were always polite and respectful with each other.

As our relationship grew, we became more involved in each other's lives. Our stories became memories from our past, our life events, and the ups and downs we have experienced. The hard, but important stuff, the lessons we learned in life.

Hundreds of phone conversations later, my neighbor and I were two peas in a pod. I could count on Helen for advice if I needed some. She was a great listener, if I needed a soundboard, just to let off steam. Helen's friendship was good therapy for me. It was good for both of us. One thing about our friendship was, I felt secure. She was honest and she never changed. She treated me the same throughout our friendship, I knew she loved me and I loved her too. We trusted each other.

A couple of years into our friendship, Helen would talk of the time when she and her husband left their families back home in Indiana and came to California to start their own family. She told me she had been twenty-seven years younger than her husband. I was shocked, she was so young.

Even with the age difference, she and her husband got along well. They worked hard and built the house she lived in. They built their house from the ground up.

I understood the two of them worked very hard. With her husband's knowledge of building and both of their elbow grease, they ended up with the perfect dwelling. When Helen talked of those days, she had a true sense of pride and accomplishment, I could almost see her smile over the phone line. I came to realize she adored her home, and it was the safest place she ever came to know. Her home was her heart.

This was Helen's first, big story from her past. She shared it with me over a couple of days. This is how her story started.

The couple traveled from out of state, and together they built their house and settled down. Helen wanted so much to start a family of her own.

In nineteen forty-three, Helen and her husband had a son. How thrilled they were to have a new baby. The newest edition to their family was, R.B. Jr.

The new baby kept Helen busy, but she loved being a mother. She explained that Jr. was an easy baby. And when he started school, he was eager to learn, he enjoyed going to school. She never had any problems with her young son. Jr. was a healthy and happy child, at that point.

When Jr. was twelve years old, Helen was pregnant for the second time. The whole family was thrilled, they were excited to have a new baby in their lives.

Helen had a joyful pregnancy. Interestingly, her best friend was pregnant at the same time. She lived in the house my parents bought many years later. The two expecting ladies ate lunch together, most days. They would laugh and dream about their baby's future. It was a wonderful time in Helen's life.

When it was time for Helen to give birth, she had some

complications. Her contractions started, she knew the baby was a girl and she was smaller than most. But Helen was still in so much pain from the labor, the doctor gave her medication to put her to sleep.

Helen woke up from her sleep, hoping to have her baby sleeping next to her. She started to panic when she didn't see or hear her baby. However, she did see her husband, and son, standing at the foot of her bed. Her husband's face was blank. He stared down at a little shoe box in his hands. The box had a name written on it's top. Helen started to cry, she knew her little Rose would never lay next to her in bed.

Helen looked at her son's face, his eyes pierced hers. He felt like it was Helen's fault the baby died. Jr. was just standing there, staring at her, blaming her with his eyes. Her heart broke.

Rose was born with underdeveloped lungs. She died during birth. A part of Helen died that day too.

My friend went into a deep depression. She did not want to face her best friend and her new baby. It was too hard for Helen to even get out of bed. All she could think about was not being able to see her little girl's face. She just wanted one look, so she could think about her, and imagine what life would be like if she had lived.

Helen's husband would not let her see her baby, Rose. Helen begged him. He stood firm on his decision.

Helen's husband died a year later, of a heart attack. Leaving Helen to raise her son alone.

MELISSA BROOKS

HOW I CRACKED THE ZODIAC'S CODE

HOW I CRACKED THE ZODIAC'S CODE

2 ABUSE

Helen started to tell me stories about her son. He was married to a lady named Lisa, and together they had eleven children. I was astonished; from being an only child to going and fathering eleven children. I struggle to understand how one woman could give birth to so many children. I know it was possible, but how could it be feasible? How could they feed all those mouths?

Helen continues to describe the children, their names, and their ages. I pictured, 'Romper Room', a kid show I watched when I was five. Just thinking about all of her grandkids exhausted me. I couldn't imagine trying to raise them all. The kids on, 'Romper Room' were able to go home to their families after the show.

Helen's tone of voice changed; grabbing my attention back to our conversation. She sounded softer but lower in pitch. And she sounded disapproving as well. What did I miss, I was daydreaming about Miss Mary Anne looking through her mirror and never saying my name. I turned my attention back to our conversation, to figure out why she had the change of voice. Helen sighed with disbelief and continued her story. I listened patiently hoping she would spit it out fast, so I could be on board. She said she couldn't believe how mean her son was to the children growing up. "He was awful," she muttered.

I was quiet, waiting for more details. She went on to say, that he treated his children so badly she could hardly admit he was her son. I waited for Helen to tell me more, and she did. She whispers, "Jr. was much harder on the girls than the boys." She did not understand why he hurt his kids. This was news to me too. I didn't see this coming after the shock of Jr. having so many children but, he abused them too? What the heck did I miss? I was trying to soak this newfound information in, and then I wondered if my friend, was too, abused by her son? She continued with shocking accounts of physical abuse her grandchildren received from their father. I was at a loss for words. My mind was racing and my heart was breaking. How does a father do this to his own flesh and blood? Why not stop having children? I was so pissed off. My thoughts went to Helen and I thought how could she let this happen?

My friend I trusted so much, I was wrong, our friendship was not real. I calmed myself and tried to think of why Helen would let this happen. Helen obviously, would not step up to her son; she had seen the terrible way he beat his children. Who knows what he would do to his Mother if she intervened? If this wasn't bad enough, Helen then tells me, her son had sexually assaulted some of his girls. I thought, some? What does that mean? She said she never saw with her own eyes, but she was positive, Jr., sexually assaulted his older girls.

I hung up the phone and I couldn't move. I was comatose, mostly in a state of shock. Did I hear right? What was Helen saying? Has she been a witness to her son's abuse to his children? How long has this been going on? Why hasn't she helped them?

I couldn't wrap my head around the whole conversation. I didn't know what to do. I decided to wait a day, I needed to calm down and I needed more information. My friend was unraveling a web of abuse, concerning her eleven grandchildren. The main abuser: her son.

HOW I CRACKED THE ZODIAC'S CODE

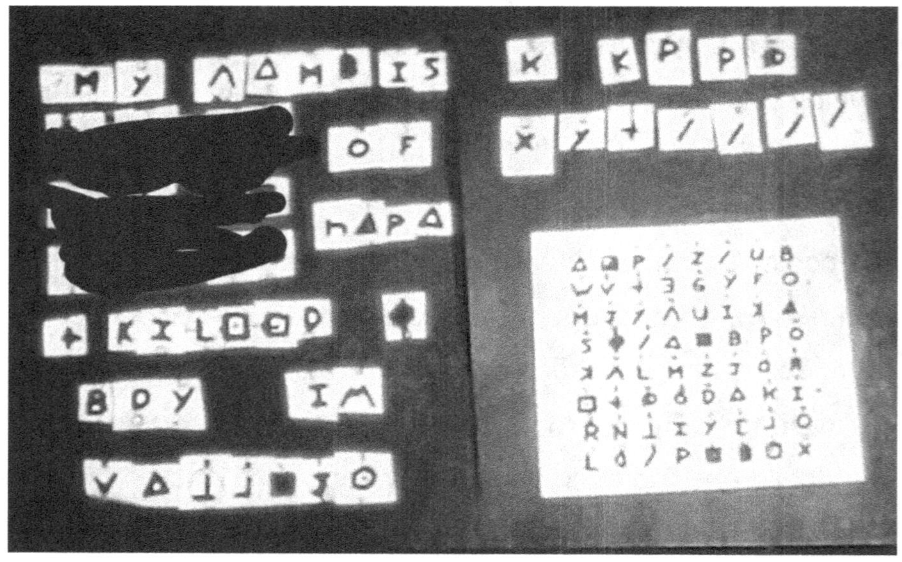

3 HIGH SCHOOL

The next day, Helen called me. I jumped up to talk to her, anticipating her call. I wasn't sure what to say, so I asked her if she was alright. She said she was, and her son and the kids had left for the day; she sounded relieved. I was horrified! Where did he go? What was he doing to them? Oh, my God! I settled down and talked to my friend, calmly.

We were on the quiet side for a few minutes, then she mentioned that on the weekends, when the kids were younger, she would take them to garage sales. It was a great way to find clothes and shoes at a good price. She could buy them all the clothes, maybe even a few outfits each.

I wondered if her son ever bought his kids books for school or took them to the movies. I highly doubted it but, I wasn't going to ask, since I was sure I knew the answers. He beat the crap out of them. Why would he buy them anything?

As I waited for Helen to end her story, I stood still and wondered what to say. Before I could even complete the thought, I heard myself asking Helen, "Does your son hurt you?" It came out of nowhere, but I wanted to know.

There was a few seconds of silence before Helen let out a slow, deep breath. "No, he doesn't hit me." Well, that's a relief. It didn't make sense but I relaxed a little, then she continued, "Jr., can sure yell at me, though." If she is only getting yelled at, she is getting off extremely easy, I said to myself. Her son only hurt kids? I was still in shock and I had the worst feeling about my near future. I was scared to know these things.

The next evening, Helen called to tell me about the time the older grandkids were taken from their father. It was the three oldest girls. On their first day of high school, the three girls were in the bathroom, combing their hair and brushing their teeth. The youngest was curling her long blonde locks; they were excited to start school, anything to get out of the house.

As the girls got ready, they forgot they weren't allowed to curl their hair. Jr. had his ways of raising his daughters; curling their hair wasn't allowed. Helen wondered how they'd even snuck in a curling iron.

The girls were being loud, and the door busted open; they were caught red-handed. One was brushing her curls, another stared at her father like a deer in headlights. All three girls ran in different directions, anywhere but towards Jr. Sheer panic filled the air. Two got away, but the youngest was grabbed by her arm and swung like a rag doll. Jr. smacked her in the face with his other hand.

She let out a shriek and tried to cover her face with her free arm. Her infuriated father yanked the curling iron out of the wall and found the first spot of bare skin he could see. He held the scorching hot iron on his daughter's bare leg for what seemed like an eternity. She let out a scream of agony. Jr. was branding his daughter like an animal on a farm; he smiled as he smelled her burnt skin.

The girl slid to the floor, holding her thigh and crying. Her father towered above her, yelling, "That's what you get for trying to be a whore." The girls had to go to school, even with the branding that hurt so much she barely could walk. She insisted on going. The first day of school was much different now that their dad messed everything up.

The three girls were silent, except for some tears quietly running down their cheeks. They separated to go to different classes and agreed to meet up at lunch. Her leg throbbed so bad it was unbearable; she asked to go to the bathroom right away. As she went through the bathroom door, her friend from the previous year smiled and went to hug her. Jr.'s younger daughter winced, afraid her wound would be accidentally touched.

The other girl asked her what was wrong, and it all came out in one long, winded answer. But the pain was hard to hide from her friend, so she just showed her the inside of her thigh. Her friend gasped in horror as she witnessed the purple burn with charred edges: that were now black. It was seeping a greenish puss in small areas; it was the size of a softball. It seriously needed medical attention.

The two girls made their way to the school nurse, and after that day, the three oldest daughters never had to live with their father again. And they never did.

4 GRANDDAUGHTER

Five years passed, and Helen and I still talked on the phone at least twice a week. I had married, moved, and had a baby. My baby was number one. Everything I did was for her; I love being a mother. Helen and I never ran out of topics to talk about.

The phone rang at my house, and it was Helen. She said one of her grandkids was coming to live with her until she could save money for an apartment. This was the girl who had been branded by her father years before. She also had a child the same age as mine. Helen's neighborhood had the best elementary school in our town. I planned on enrolling my kid in this school, so Helen's great-grandkid would also be enrolled there.

School started and the kids were in the same class. I ended up becoming friends with Helen's granddaughter. I liked her right away; we both had so many things in common. It wasn't hard to be friends. Our kids would play at my parent's house after school sometimes. After getting to know Helen's granddaughter, I noticed her personality would change; like she was an entirely different girl. All of the personalities made me think of a book I read when I was younger, called, 'Sybil'. The little girl in the story was so abused as a child, she ended up having multiple personalities. Sixteen, to be exact. This was a true story.

I was pretty sure, Helen's granddaughter, had several different personalities. I witnessed five. I cared for Helen and all of her family. They had been through a different upbringing, unfortunately. I still was amazed at the bizarre altercations we endeavored.

A few years had passed and our girls were still in school together. I had moved in with my father, so I was Helen's neighbor again.

Some odd things happened when I was Helen's neighbor. One year during summer, I threw a birthday party for my daughter. I invited her friends from school; the parents just needed to drop off their kids and come back in three hours to pick them up.

It was a success. Everyone had a great time. As the last two kids were waiting for their parents, I cleaned up the mess from the party. Only one kid left, and it was Helen's great-granddaughter; that was easy, I could walk her home.

My telephone rang; it was Helen's granddaughter. She would be late, thirty more minutes. I said, "Okay; no problem."

As I looked around the room, I noticed someone was missing-the little girl. I had a horrible feeling, this was going to be hard, first, finding her and then, sending her home with her mom. If her Mom showed up.

I searched high and low; I could not find her. Maybe she walked home; I called Helen, and she had not seen her. I called her name over and over. She was playing with me. I was not playing anymore. Then, I heard her faint, little giggle. I could not see her. She was good at this game of hide-and-seek.

It was two hours from the time her mom called. This was getting very old and I just wanted this child to listen to me. Who was I kidding, this child would hardly listen to her mom.

So, I tricked her, I pretended I gave up on the search for her. I acted like I was getting ready for bed. She couldn't stand being ignored. She darted past me and I didn't react. I acted like I didn't even see her. I knew she would do it again. I was right, she flew by me, and this time she got closer. When she was close enough to me; I just reached out and grabbed her arm and held on tight. She was small, but she was strong; I could barely hold onto her.

This little girl was wiggling, spasin' out, trying so hard to get out of my arms. The child was kicking and screaming at me. I was not letting go; I did not care how hard she tried to get away. I struggled to get to the front gate, and with her still in my grasp, I made it to the gate. The gate suddenly opened, and there was her Mom, on the other side. The little girl jumped out of my arms and into her mother's.

Boy, did she turn into an instant angel? I gasped, in shock at her acting skills. I said, "Thanks for coming, see you girls later." I turned around and went back to my house. I was wiped out. One little girl wore me out. I could not believe how strong she was. She fought me for twenty minutes, at least. When I went to bed, I looked at my arms and legs; I looked like a truck had run over me. I had bruises from head to toe. I was amazed at the damage she caused; to my body, and the level of stress she created at my house; she acted like she didn't have a care in the world. Well, I guess she didn't.

This would be another incident I had that involved Helen's granddaughter and great-granddaughter.

School had started. I picked up my kid from school and went straight home. We were still living at my parent's house.

As my daughter and I walked into the house, this wave of putrid aroma hit our noses. Whoa, what the heck was that smell? What in the world died in here? It was horrible. We turned and ran out the front door.

The smell was so foul, I imagined my two pit bulls were

hanging by their necks, in my kitchen. With their insides hanging out. My parent's house wreaked of death. My daughter and I could barely stay inside for a minute, then we had to go back outside for some fresh air.

I tried to find where the smell was coming from, but I couldn't find anything.

After hours of airing out the house, and scrubbing the walls and floors, the phone rang.

It was my neighbor, Helen, who was apologizing for her granddaughter's behavior. I didn't know what she was talking about. She continued to say, what had happened earlier in the day. Helen's granddaughter kept her daughter home from school. Instead, they went to the river, to go fishing. The river ran behind our houses; it was close by. As the girls walked by my house, they thought it would be funny to throw the old, smelly, rotten sardines, they were using to fish with, in my parent's front door. They thought it was humorous, but I thought it was disgusting, and pretty inconvenient, too.

I never understood why they did this, I took it personally and it hurt my feelings. In time, I realized it wasn't me or my daughter that they were attacking. It was the way Helen's granddaughter was raised, the abuse she survived, and the effect it must have had on her and her daughter. Their outlandish behavior was the result of their abuse.

I spoke to Helen and told her it was okay, and not to worry. I knew she had enough of their mischievous behavior, she was getting tired of it.

This was another incident, but a different day. It was nighttime and I was at my parent's house. I heard a gunshot, it was super close by. I heard a vehicle take off fast, wheels squealing. A woman's voice, sounded like Helen's granddaughter, very drunk. She was shouting lots of mother f-er's and some slurred ones I didn't understand.

Five minutes had passed, and one of my girlfriends opened my front door, yelling, "Hide these, hide these!" I grabbed what was in her hand, and it was bullets. I started to make my version of the story because I heard the gun, the car, and the screaming.

My girlfriend told me it was Helen's granddaughter shooting at the man who gave her a ride home from the bar. I don't know what happened but he almost got a bullet in his head, he is lucky he got away.

No one was hurt, by the grace of God.

The final story involving Helen's granddaughter, was when one of my dogs escaped my yard. He went next store to check out the chickens, that were running around the yard. The chickens belonged to Helen's granddaughter. She let them run free in Helen's yard. This was a new smell for my dog. He ended up chasing one of the chickens and killing it.

Helen's granddaughter told me, she was holding my dog hostage in her basement until she got a ride to the pound. She wanted my dog to go to jail, for killing her chicken. She wanted my dog to die, too. I understood she was upset, and I was sorry it happened, but I asked her, "Can I have my dog, now?"

She kept my dog for sixteen hours, with no water, or food, tied up in Helen's basement. Finally, Helen made her granddaughter return my dog.

The next day Helen's granddaughter and great-granddaughter were gone. I wondered where they went. Months later, Helen told me her son put his daughter in a mental hospital. Her child went to live with the child's father. It was sad to hear, and I wish she could have had an easier life. Now, she was locked up and taken from her daughter. It was sad.

Weeks passed and Helen told me she went with her son to visit her granddaughter. They drove a few hours away and took her out to dinner. Helen brought her cigarettes, too. She said they went to Sizzler to have dinner. All three of them were sitting at a table. Her granddaughter was extra mouthy that night. She continually made rude comments to her father, implying he was a terrible father, and that he was abusive to her sisters and brothers. She hated him for those reasons.

Jr. had heard enough; he pushed his chair out and stood up. He started for the exit. His dinner sat untouched on the table. He rushed out the door and went to his car. He was not going to wait very long either. They had to leave the restaurant without eating.

HOW I CRACKED THE ZODIAC'S CODE

28

HOW I CRACKED THE ZODIAC'S CODE

5 THE BABYSITTER

On this day, Helen and I had a long conversation on the telephone. This was a story from her and Jr.'s past. He was in Kindergarten, so he must have been five years old. Helen did not say where her husband was, but he was not around at this time. Jr. had a friend over the house to play after school. Helen had the day off, so she could let the kids play outside, then feed them dinner, and do any homework they might have. Then Helen would drive Jr.'s friend home. It was a well-thought-out plan.

HOW I CRACKED THE ZODIAC'S CODE

The fun day did not go as planned. It turned into a real nightmare for Helen and the boys. As the kids played outside, Helen's phone rang. She picked up the phone and immediately regretted it. It was Helen's work. They needed her to come in and do a split shift. Somebody called in sick, so they were understaffed. Helen hung up the phone and had to tell the boys something came up and the play date would be ending. She was called into work.

As the kids huffed and puffed because they still wanted to play, Helen felt bad that their plans had to change. If she only had a babysitter for the afternoon, that would let Helen go to work and then be able to spend the latter part of the day with the kids. She turned the pages of her phonebook quickly, hoping to find someone to babysit. Suddenly, the doorbell chimed. Who on earth could this be? Helen swung open the front door to be face-to-face with Gerald, the homeless man in town. Gerald was always kind when he spoke to Helen. He even asked her if she needed any help mowing the lawn or taking out the trash. Helen hesitated, then asked how he felt about watching the kids for a couple of hours. She would pay him by the hour. Gerald happily agreed, and off Helen went to work. She would see the boys that afternoon.

Helen pulled up to her house three hours later. She had worked her shift and now was ready to feed the kids. As she was walking up the front walk, she stopped. Is that crying I hear? Starting to feel nervous, she hurried along the walkway and entered her house. Oh, what a sight! Two five-year-old boys without clothes on. Their faces were covered in dirt, and so were their knees. The boys were crying; they did not even glance towards Helen's voice. They had their heads down in shame, and tears were running down their dirty faces.

Helen exploded, screaming at the top of her lungs, and frantically looking for the sitter. "Gerald, how could you touch these innocent children? Don't you ever come back to this house again!" She was running in and out of the rooms, looking intensely for this man. She heard the front door slam and knew it was Gerald leaving.

All Helen could do was clean the boys up, feed them dinner, and do their homework with them. After the day the babysitter molested the two five-year-olds, the situation was never brought up again. The cops were not called, and the parents of Jr.'s friend were never told of the sexual abuse. It had been ignored and shoved under the rug. Helen acted like it never happened. Maybe that was good for Helen, but it was not good for the boys. They carried around pain and fear from that terrible day; they felt the shame and humiliation that come with abuse.

How the inner turmoil the boys must have had all those years; all the feelings of anger and guilt could turn anyone into a serial killer. As I listened to this distant memory, I tensed up at the thought of the confusion that must have gone through the boys' minds, so many years ago.

Helen said in those days, in the mid-to-late forties, no one talked about sexual abuse. People did it, but it was not talked about. Helen never told anyone. My heart went out to the boys; Gerald took away their innocence. They looked at the world through pain agony and worthlessness.

After she finished the story, she told me she never talked about it because it brought the wrong kind of attention to families. She kept quiet about the incident, fearing it would bring harm to her and her son. The last words she chose to say to me that day were, "Gerald was the Devil himself, he was pure evil."

When I heard about this predator, raping these little boys, I began to wonder about the Zodiac's unsolved case. This type of brutality on children, damages lives forever. The idea of not being able to work through what happened and trying to cope with the feelings alone would result in disaster.

The boys had never talked about it to anyone; they must have been emotionally stunted by this incident. Their feelings of anger and betrayal, bottled up inside, must have found a way out.

More and more, my feelings about Jr. and how he might be the Zodiac haunted me every day. There were too many signs, for me to ignore the facts. It seemed I would hear something every day to further my belief, that this was true. The information points to Helen's son, making it more and more possible for him to be the infamous serial killer.

MELISSA BROOKS

HOW I CRACKED THE ZODIAC'S CODE

6 ZODIAC

A few months had passed. Our conversations were short and sweet most of the time. The last story of the babysitter abusing the boys was a game-changer for me. I was sure Jr. was the one.

The next significant bit of information was when Helen called me in the afternoon. She had asked me one question: "How could a man go hunting every other weekend in a year, and not bring home one kill from the hunt? Not one animal? No deer, no duck, not even a rabbit." Helen asked me if I thought that was strange, and I agreed it was.

So Jr. was a hunter; he had guns. I knew he had at least

one gun- remember, I hid the bullets. I was thinking about something Helen told me once. She said one of her grandkids could take a gun apart, clean it, and put it back together. Without help from an adult. This kid was three years old.

My mind was racing with so many thoughts. I also remember her saying, her son was a weapons specialist in the military. He served in the Reserves every other weekend. So, he would go hunting one weekend with no animals to ever prove it, and the following weekends, he would serve in the Reserves.

Another interesting question Helen asked about her son, was why someone would serve in the military for years and never take a pay upgrade. He never wanted to change his rank. Yes, this was odd; who doesn't want more money? If he just wanted the privileges the military offers, like access to special stores military bases always have a P.X., a tax-free store that sells special military items. They have a huge range of items for military personnel and their families. So, this would be a legitimate reason for staying in the military and not furthering his career or wallet. He could use the facilities and be under the radar. Her son had access to any military base across the country.

At this time, I was very interested in the unsolved Zodiac case. I started doing my research and looked up as much as I could find on this case. I found lots of information on the F.B.I. website. I started reading everything I could come across. This is what I found:

The first murder the Zodiac admitted to, was down in Southern California. It was a brutal murder of a pretty young girl who was studying at the Riverside library. The Zodiac walked into the library with a plan to kill. He knew who his target was; a young, pretty girl studying at the library that day. He knew she pulled up in a Volkswagen Beetle; he also already tampered with her car. He had to make sure she couldn't leave and he could be the one to rescue her. He took her distributor cap off, making it impossible to start. Then he sat back and waited for her to leave. As he waited, the Zodiac etched a poem into one of the library's wooden desktops, with the tip of his knife. When the girl left the library, of course, she couldn't start her car. The Zodiac approached her and asked if she needed some help. He already knew the answer, but he continued to offer her a ride. The young girl agreed to get a ride. He pointed in the direction of his car; they started to walk towards his vehicle. They had to walk between some empty houses. As they approached the alleyway, he said something to her, like, "Are you ready to die?" She looked as if she didn't know what he meant. Then, he brutally attacked her with such force he nearly decapitated the innocent girl. He used a knife. The girl put up a fight because there was a ripped watchband at the crime scene. The police also found blonde hair and skin under her fingernails. Other items were also found in the alleyway. The police took pictures of footprints at the crime scene. The footprints were from a pair of special Air Force Wing Walker boots. They were a size ten and a half. The watchband found, was a men's, size seven. The special boots could only be purchased at a P.X., post exchange, on a military base. The other item in evidence at the Riverside Police Department was a wooden desktop, with a poem etched into its top.

With all of this new information from the Zodiac case online, I dug deeper and looked up military bases close to the library. There were three bases, within forty-five miles. The first one was five minutes away- March Air Force Base. That was close, five minutes or less, in a car.

I started to think, how could I find out where someone was living, way back in nineteen sixty-eight?

I sat at my computer and typed in Helen's son's name. Boy, was I surprised, that multiple links came back from the search. I clicked on one of the links and official documents appeared on my screen. They were marriage certificates. This was interesting, Helen's son had been married twice.

The first time was with a lady in Riverside, California. They were married for a year and had a child. A boy! He gave the boy his name. The marriage did not last. They were divorced in one year. To my surprise, the divorce was final the same month the Zodiac admitted to killing the girl from the library.

The next link I clicked on was a webpage that was trying to sell a video. The video was lessons to teach you self-defense. Supposedly, Helen's son wrote a testimonial for this technique. I read further, trying to see where his name was on the page. And then I saw it, the scope and crosshairs symbol. It was on the cover of the video. If this didn't tie the two together, what would?

It was another thing to convince me I was on to him.

As I looked at the F.B.I. case files, there were the original letters the Zodiac wrote in the seventies. This crosshairs symbol was used many times. It was considered his trademark.

The white crosshair symbol was sewn onto a black hood. The Zodiac wore this when he hid behind a tree in Lake Berryessa, Northern California. He was spying on a couple who were having a picnic by the lake. The female noticed him first, and she told her male friend, they had a visitor. The Zodiac slowly emerged from behind the tree and started to walk towards the couple. The man stood up and offered the hooded man all the money he had in his wallet. The Zodiac said no, he didn't want money. He tossed the female some rope and told her to tie up her friend. She did what she was told, but she tied the rope loosely, so perhaps he could escape from the ropes. The Zodiac caught on and tied her up tight and tightened the man's ropes too. The Zodiac proceeded to stab the woman many times then moved over to the man. The couple lay there in miserable pain. The hooded man walked away. As the sun went down the couple lay in their blood and started screaming for help. A fisherman passed by and thought he heard something. He turned his boat around and went closer to the shore. It was dark so it was hard to see. The fisherman took out his flashlight and scanned the shore. His light stopped on the two people covered in blood. They were in agony. The fisherman quickly went to get help. A ranger and the fisherman found the couple by the shore. The woman was in so much pain she was barely able to talk. The ranger called the ambulance, which was still going to take thirty minutes to reach the couple. The man who was stabbed didn't think she would make it to the hospital. But they both did, unfortunately, the woman died two days later in the hospital. The man survived. The woman was attacked more violently than the man.

Later the police found evidence of footprints by the couple's car. They appeared to be the same prints as the ones at the library, in Southern California. They also found the writing on the couple's car stating the dates when other murders took place. The Zodiac was now admitting to more of his crimes. That evening the Zodiac used a pay phone and called the police in Napa. He talked to a dispatcher. He said he wanted to report two murders up at the lake. He then admitted to killing the two kids the year before.

Now, as I look at the symbol again, I think no way, this is too easy. Being curious about what was being sold to the public, I scoured the website. I did checks on who made the website, who it was registered to, who wrote the book, and who made the video for the merchandise being sold. I read and reread the testimonials for the video/book being sold and the reviews kind of had a familiar tone to them. Like I have read something similar. Almost like Deja Vu.

I kept reading the reviews over and over, especially the one written by Helen's Son. I thought, the nerve of this man, to first, kill innocent people, and second, make money off of them.

Then I realized, that Helen's son was the author of the entire website. He fabricated the whole site. He was trying to sell self-defense classes.

I kept looking on the site for more clues and I found some.

When the police found the two kids in Benicia, on Lake Herman Rd. One of the reports in the newspaper said this killer must have been a marksman. He shot dead aim at his target while she was running away in the dark. The Zodiac replied to this by writing a letter to the police department stating he was not a marksman he just taped a pen flashlight to his gun scope. He would point the gun in the direction of his target and when the light hit it he would shoot.

Going back to the video being sold online. I read in a testimonial the same comment. It said, taping a flashlight to your gun scope would give you perfect aim in the dark.

I ran across a few clips of the video on the same website. A few people were giving examples of defending one's self. I was shocked.

I was watching real footage of a man shooting a rifle as he casually walked at a slow pace. The person in the video was Helen's son!

I had to catch my breath. It was a surreal moment for me. I was scared.

HOW I CRACKED THE ZODIAC'S CODE

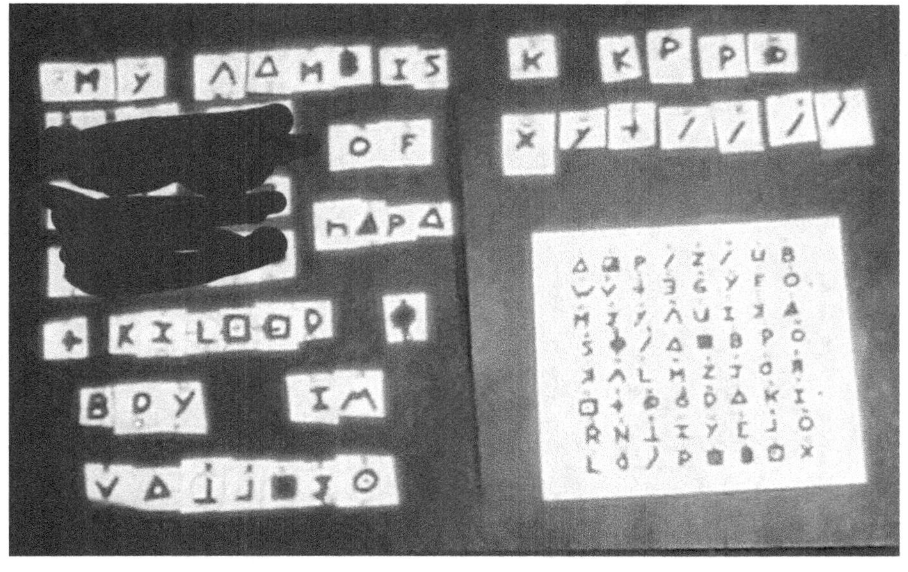

HOW I CRACKED THE ZODIAC'S CODE

7 THE DINNER DATE

There was a day when Helen said to me, that she got a phone call from Jr.'s ex-wife and she was upset, she told Helen that her son was the Zodiac. I asked why would she say that. Helen said the ex said he was never home when the murders happened. Helen seemed shocked to hear her son could be a serial killer, I cringed.

Helen went on to say her son's ex was mad because she was cut out of the will. The grandkids were cut out too.
I listened to her and kept my mouth shut. All I heard was, that Jr. was the Zodiac. The hairs on my neck stood straight up.

Weeks had passed and Helen called me one night and said

her son was picking her up the next day. He was going to take her to dinner. She was reluctant to go, she felt nervous about the whole situation.

She said her son insisted she go, she had no choice. Helen said she would call me when she returned.

I waited for her phone call, but it never came. I started to worry about my friend. She always called me. It seemed like hours and hours had passed. Still no call from Helen.

I went to bed at eleven and I still hadn't heard from her.

The next day she did call me. Helen sounded awful. Her voice was low and she was whispering. She sounded so sad, I asked her what was wrong. She began to tell me what had happened.

Helen's son picked her up to take her to dinner. They drove three hours away, to go to dinner. She had wished they could have stayed in town. He insisted they go to the town where he lived. After the long drive, they pull up to a retirement facility. This is where they had dinner. The dinner was not very special either, she wondered why he chose this place. After dinner, he walked her down a hallway to an apartment door. Jr. pulled out a key and opened the door. Helen's heart dropped, her furniture was set up just like at her house. Her furniture was there in this apartment set up exactly like it was at her house. She felt sick, he had tricked her. While they ate dinner someone moved all her furniture and items from her house and moved them to this apartment three hours away.

Helen found her bed and collapsed on it. She passed out in

tears, knowing she would never live in her house again.

The line went quiet, I was in shock, how could her son do this to her? This was low, what a cowardly thing to do. My heart went out to my friend.

I recognized Helen never talked of her house, or took pride in building it, after her move.

Jr. decided to rent out his Mother's house. I suppose for the extra income, which I am sure, Helen never received any of the money.

So Jr.'s plan had worked, he had control of everything, her bank account and her house. Meanwhile, Helen was miserable living three hours away from everything she knew.

Helen still called me every day. I could tell she was depressed and lonely. We talked on the phone more than usual.

She had said, yes, Jr. had put his name on her bank account. She felt helpless. She would mention how she had a lawyer friend and she wished she would call him and ask his advice. She was too scared of her son's rebuttal, so she never called her friend.

During this time, Jr. was sticking a 'For Rent' sign in Helen's front yard. Two of my girlfriends saw the sign and instantly called the number in hopes of renting Helen's house.

I had explained to my girlfriend what had happened to Helen. No matter her despair, they jumped at the chance to rent the house.

The day had come to meet up with Jr. and talk about renting

Helen's house. My girlfriends went together and quietly waited for Jr. to arrive. When he pulled up to the house he took out a toolbox and and walked through the back door. My friends waited on the front porch. Twenty minutes later he let them in. Jr. walked around like he was busy fixing things or changing lightbulbs. My girlfriends waited patiently. Finally, he decided to talk to them. As he asked them a few questions and he was listening to their responses, the front door flew open with a vengeance. It was a thirty-year-old white woman screaming profanities. My friends looked on in shock not sure what was happening. This red-faced short blonde lady went on and on about how she knew what he did to those people. This woman was pointing in Jr.'s direction and walking toward him too. Jr. jumped up grabbed his toolbox and exited the house, out the backdoor. My friends explained to me Jr. turned white as a ghost when this lady started saying these things to him. But he didn't say a word just vacated as fast as he could. They never saw him again.

My two girlfriends asked me every day have you asked Helen what was going on? I told them every day I was not going to bother her with those questions she was already so upset about her house.

Two weeks later a rental property company put the house up for rent and Jr. had nothing to do with renting it out anymore.

I found out who the crazy lady who barged into Helen's house was months later. It was a childhood friend of one of

Jr.'s daughters. They were friends when they were little, I suppose elementary school age.

This childhood friend knew some dirt on Jr. and I wondered what it was. I am sure it wasn't good. I had tried to reach this girl months later but she had moved to the city and she was in a program for alcoholics. I could never get enough information to contact her, but I did try.

Even though this happened with my friends and Jr. I just said they could try to go through the rental company if they still wanted to rent Helen's home.

Helen and I were still talking multiple times a week. She had mentioned she was so homesick. She was so lonely too, I told her I would drive up and see her in the next few days. This made her happy and it made me happy too.

I went to visit Helen and she was delighted. I sat in her little kitchen with her and talked for hours. During my visit, her son popped up out of the blue. He extended his hand to me and I grabbed his hand and shook it firmly. I thought his hand felt like a vampire's hand, cold as ice. He even had the coloring of one, his skin was white as snow with blue undertones. I felt goosebumps all over and my face turned red because I could feel the heat on my face. I quickly sat back down and continued to talk with my friend.

Helen said it was odd how he just showed up when I was there. She said she had not seen him in days then he just appeared at her apartment.

I returned home soon after I met Helen's son. He made me

nervous and he creeped me out. I did tell Helen I would come back and pick her up. So she could visit with me and her one friend she had in town. She would always talk of this friend of hers, she had known her for many years. She could visit her house, which she missed so much. This made Helen happy and I couldn't wait to go back to her apartment to pick her up.

A few weeks later I did just that. I drove to her apartment picked her up and we headed back to my town. We had a great time, the drive seemed short because we talked the whole way. I took her to see her friend and we went to my house too. By this time I had moved across town so Helen's house was not my neighbor anymore. But we did park by her old house and just talked, looking at her house. This made her feel really good. I felt good doing this for her.

It was getting late so we went through a drive-thru and we ordered hamburgers and fries for the ride home. We had a wonderful time talking all day. Believe it or not, after we ate we still chatted the whole way back to her apartment.

We said our goodbyes and we cried a little too. I hoped to see her again soon.

8 HOSPITALIZED

Months had passed and Helen and I talked at least once a week. But this one time when she called me she was terrified. I asked her what was happening. She said Jr. had just driven her to a hospital and left her. She was not sure why she was there, she was not sick. She was scared. Helen told me the nurse who was taking her to a room had taken her purse. This was very upsetting to her. Her wallet and her phonebook were in her purse. These are the two items that she has to have with her at all times. She was confused about the whole situation. She told me she felt like Jr. was doing this to her to keep her away from me and her running around doing what she wanted. He did not trust me or his Mother.

I did not know what to say or do, I felt helpless. Helen told me thank goodness she had my phone number memorized or she wouldn't have been able to call me. I felt a little relief that I could talk to her and try and calm her down. I had no idea what her son was up to now. As we were talking quietly she heard the nurse coming into her room, she said she had to hang up now. I told her I loved her then the line went silent.

I sat and cried for my friend for a long time. I felt useless like I could not help her. This was terrible and I know she was scared and alone.

All I could do was wait for her to call me back from wherever she was. I waited and waited, hoping to hear from her soon.

After months had passed I finally realized that Helen was not going to call me. I was so upset that she never called, what had happened to her? How could her son do this?

I decided to google Helen's name on my computer. What popped up devastated me, it was her obituary. Helen had passed away on my birthday, two months earlier.

I stared in disbelief at my computer screen and cried. Was this real, did my friend die on my birthday? I knew deep down she did.

After some time passed and I began to deal with my friend's death, I started thinking of all the conversations Helen and I had over the years.

I began to think of her son and his abusive behavior. I was going to do some digging on his background. I was curious about what I could find on him.

I googled his name again and looked into the web pages I had found before. It was so bizarre to see the Zodiac symbol on a webpage and his name on the same website. There had to be a connection. I felt it, so I just kept looking up different things about the Zodiac and comparing them with the information I already knew about Helen's Son.

I turned my attention to the infamous Zodiac ciphers. There were lots of people trying to solve these ciphers but no one has found the answers.

I felt like I knew one piece of information that no one else had, I knew his true name. It was my goal to try and figure out the ciphers, I could do it because I had his name and his address.

I printed out a few ciphers from the F.B.I. website. I began with the three-forty-degree cipher. This was the biggest one, so I started with it.

I remember reading what the Zodiac said to the editors of the major newspapers. He said print these ciphers on your front pages or I will go on a killing spree. He also said if the ciphers could be solved they would show his identity and his address.

I took the information I already knew some of the answers and I took the letters out of the cipher and spelled his name.

As I went back over the Zodiac case files I read that the Zodiac also said if these ciphers were not printed on the front pages of the newspapers he would go on a killing spree knocking the little kiddies off as they exited the school buses.

HOW I CRACKED THE ZODIAC'S CODE

The public panicked, holding their children close. Society locked their doors and prayed they were not next on his list.

The Zodiac had people everywhere scared to live their normal lives. He had everyone terrified. This was happening in nineteen sixty-eight and sixty-nine.

It was an uneasy time: people were looking over their shoulders. No one felt safe in their homes and on the streets. Who was going to be next?

The police were clueless, they did not know who was committing the murders. The Zodiac had everyone fooled.

Three different police stations were covering the Zodiac case in the seventies. The police stations did not share information about the case. This made it impossible to get further into the case, much less get close to solving it.

The Zodiac's elaborate way of communicating with the public and his pursuers still captivates crime buffs today.

There are thousands of Zodiac followers from around the world online. Some people get together every year to discuss the Zodiac case. The group meets near one of the crime scenes. They hope to talk about any new evidence that has come up on the case. They are hoping to solve the Zodiac mystery.

People who lived during the Zodiac killings wanted answers too, they needed answers. Society felt cheated, they worried about their children going to school. The public did not feel safe walking down the street. No one would go outside at night. Everyone locked their doors.

There were movies made about the Zodiac murders but, they did not answer the real questions. They wanted to know who this killer was, and what kind of life did he have? What drove him to commit these horrific killings?

The movies that were made about the Zodiac killings portrayed a man they thought was the killer. They were incorrect.

There was a man who was blamed for the Zodiac killings but, the only item that tied him to the Zodiac case was a watch this man's Mother gave him. It was a zodiac watch. The watch had the name Zodiac on its face, that was the only evidence the police had on this man who was innocent of these crimes.

The different novels written about the Zodiac Killer had the wrong guy too.

Society had to know who the real killer was, and he was still out there walking around free to kill again.

I too was scared of this man. When I was spending time researching the data on this case, I had nightmares, thinking this man was crouching in the corner of my room ready to attack me.

HOW I CRACKED THE ZODIAC'S CODE

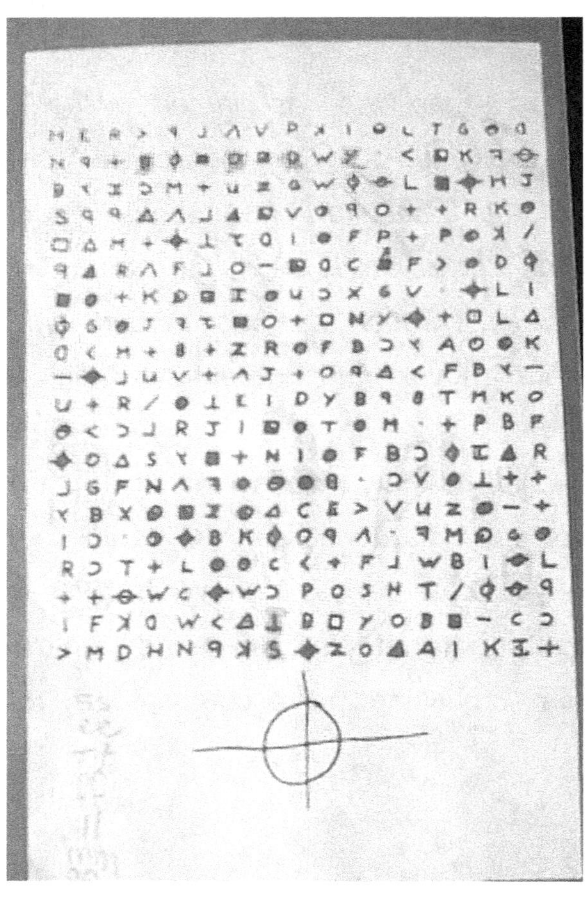

9 CIPHERS

I had a few different Zodiac novels and I read them more than a few times. This one particular book had printed the three-forty-degree cipher on one of the pages. For some reason, I could not stop looking at this image. I would look at it for hours hoping something would click and I would be able to understand it. This is how I figured out the message.

I thought back to when the Zodiac stated whoever cracks my code will have my true identity. Now to get his true identity would be to know who he was to begin with. Otherwise, no one would be able to crack his ciphers.

I went to the F.B.I. website again and printed copies of

this particular cipher. I printed perhaps ten copies of it. I then began marking one of the copies with a pencil. I was circling letters and crossing out symbols. Erasing my pencil marks and my scribbling I had done all over the page. It was for sure a mess. So I grabbed another printed-out cipher and then circled the letters of the name I was confident was to blame for the murders.

Then I thought of another way to solve this cipher. First I would cut all the letters out individually. Then stack them in piles. Of course, I put them in alphabetical order too. When I finished this task I went on to take letters from the piles that I already knew.

I began with the name and then took the letters to write out the address I knew for certain was my neighbor's address. This was the way I ended up solving the cipher.

I then went over the letters from the case files. I pulled letters to copy his exact wording from the letters he wrote the public and the police. For example, I AM THE ZODIAC, I LIVE IN ANY TOWN. This was getting me nervous and excited at the same time. I thought this was too easy. I continued to use the same words the Zodiac used years before in his written letters. I just kept going until I used almost every letter in the cipher.

I then tried the other ciphers available online. I used the same system as I did on the first one. And finally, I completed four of the Zodiac ciphers. I felt pretty pleased.

Like I said the only way I was able to crack the Zodiac's

code was because I knew his name.

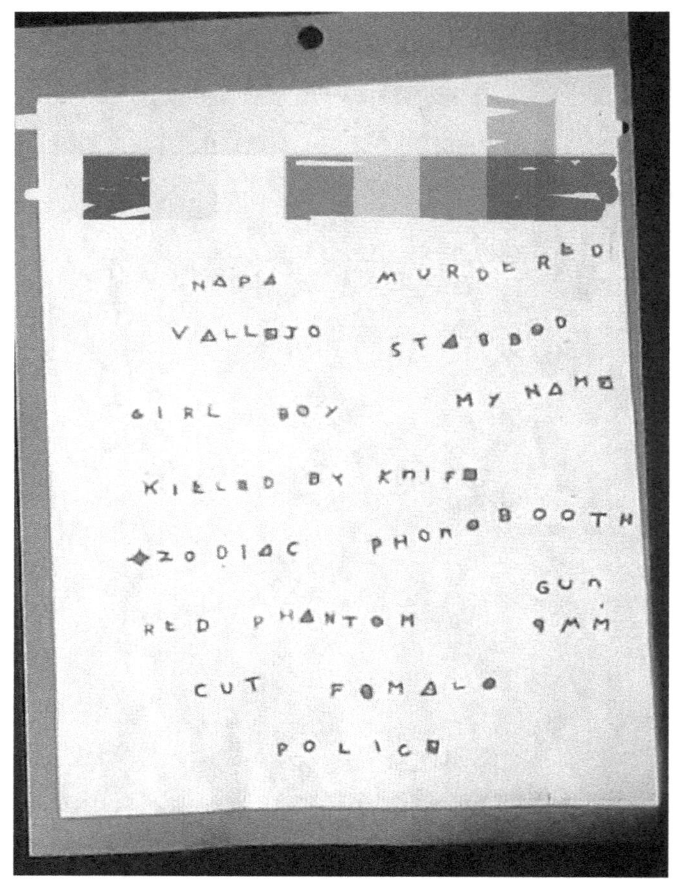
NAPA   MURDERED
VALLEJO   STABBED
GIRL   BOY   MY NAME
KILLED BY KNIFE
ZODIAC   PHONE BOOTH
                    GUN
RED PHANTOM   9MM
CUT   FEMALE
POLICE

MELISSA BROOKS

HOW I CRACKED THE ZODIAC'S CODE

10 F.B.I.

I completed four ciphers. Now was the time to decide what to do with the information. In my mind, I solved the Zodiac mystery, I should then show the authorities.

I contemplated calling the local police first. They would appreciate my findings, right? Well not necessarily.

I called the police department and asked to speak to a detective. Once I was on the phone with one, I told him my story and wanted to know if he would like me to mail him my solved ciphers. He said yes and he would return my call after six weeks.

Ten weeks went by and I received his call. He explained that he called the man in question's ex-wife and she did admit there was a very violent background and a definite military background. But, it was all circumstantial evidence. The detective also told me, you can pull any name out of the ciphers.

The detective's attitude and tone were rude and short. I tried to explain how Helen's Son had forged her name on her bank account. He tells me this happens every day it is called elder abuse. He then hung up the phone with a quick goodbye.

I was flabbergasted, I sat there for a minute just recapping what had just happened. Unbelievable, what a joke.

The call from the police was a bummer. I decided to call the F.B.I. They might be interested in my detective work.

I found that looking up the number was easy but talking to a real person was hard. I called the F.B.I. office a few times. Finally, someone answered. He took my information and said to wait for a return call. I waited and waited. The call did come and I was instantly nervous. My voice was shaky and I felt like he was not taking me seriously. He did ask me some questions and I answered the best I could. Like the police Detective, this agent was quick to get off the phone. The call ended.

As I sat and thought about the call I felt defeated. The agent told me people call every day with crazy stories of the Zodiac. The calls never pan out. He sounded like he had no patience for my call.

I was not happy with the results from the F.B.I. office. So I then decided to call another office in a bigger city.

This time I spoke to an agent right away. He told me he

would have another agent call me back to set up an appointment. I was thrilled.

A month passed and another agent did call me. We set a time and date for me to go into his office. I was very nervous.

A week later my Mom and I were sitting in an agent's office waiting to be seen.

Two agents walked in and introduced themselves and were very polite. I started to tell my story and showed them my ciphers.

These agents seemed interested and were very friendly. By the time my Mom and I left they were explaining how they went to the movie premiere with one of the victims of the Zodiac. The one gentleman from the lake.

The F.B.I. agents told me they appreciated me coming in and sharing this information. They also said they would not be able to contact me about the case.

We said our goodbyes and my Mom and I went home.

A few years passed and I still thought of the case every day and of my friend, Helen. I had moved in with my Mother to help care for her. I saw my friend's house every day.

One day as I was looking out the window staring at Helen's house, a man walked in the back door. He never even looked in my direction he was stoned-faced, like a robot. As I heard the back door of Helen's house slam I realized who the man was.

It was Jr., Helen's Son.

Chills went down my spine.

LEGAL DISCLOSURE

The names and places may have been changed to protect the

innocent families involved.

SENSITIVE DISCLOSURE

Warning, graphic, and violent material. Please know

information from a real criminal unsolved case has been

included.

The author is telling her story from her perspective and

experience.